Coywolf

Antonio Bellia (Madly Loved)

Coywolf

Copyright © 2018 by Antonio Bellia (Madly Loved)

Published by Local Gems Press

www.localgemspoetrypress.com

To every living creature who has
overcome adversity through
persistence, determination, and courage

Foreword

Since I was a child I had a fascination with wolves. I liked everything about them: their social life, their looks, their agility and majestic appearance. Their eyes had a hypnotic effect, even in a photo or a movie. I had never seen one in real life.

I dreamed of finding a wolf puppy and raising him to be my best friend, but of course that did not happen.

Growing up I continued to read articles about wolves, and to watch every White Fang movie I could. Eventually I realized that wolves had been persecuted almost to extinction.

Sleepless one night, rather than count sheep to fall asleep, I flipped channels. I stopped when a documentary titled *Coywolf* had the completely opposite effect. It woke me up.

Was I understanding this right? Scientists had determined that the "coyotes" people had seen in towns and cities were not in fact coyotes. Research revealed wolves and coyotes had mated and a new creature had been born: the coywolf.

Why? Why would a wolf and a coyote mate?

My imagination was ignited.

Table of Contents

I

It was a dark night. The trees in the forest were bowing in all directions, moved by a disorderly and merciless wind. An icy rain violently whipped the forest, and the lightning glamorously announced the powerful thunder: a messenger of the gods above declaring ownership and dominion over all that is below and all there is above.

All the creatures found shelter, squirrels in their hollow trees, birds in their nests, fox in its den.

All had found their places except an old wolf still running through the storm toward his cave, toward his pack, and a man, disappointed to have missed his target, staggering along on the wet soggy floor of that dark forest.

Now the man could see the warm light of a fire escaping from the fire pit; a door opened, a group of little humans and a woman welcomed him. As he stepped into the dry warm room he laid his gun down. The woman took his wet jacket from his back and he walked to a chair near the fire. He sat down and as he began to take his boots off, the children impatiently asked him: "Did you get him, did you get him?"

The father looked at them soberly and when his second boot was off, began to tell the story: "No, I could not get him, but I was so close to him I could see his breath steaming out of his nostrils. His eyes were like fire, his fangs were sharp and strong enough to tear apart a buffalo. At the loud sound of my shotgun, with one leap he disappeared into the black of the forest, but as I was walking back the sound of his breath followed me all the way here."

"O, honey," the sweet voice of his wife interrupted, saying, "You are frightening the children," as she put her arms around their shoulders.

Then, while being escorted to their bedroom, one of the boys, with his eyes still filled with images of the story, soberly said, "Momma, I'm not afraid. . .when I grow up I'm going to kill that big bad wolf.

When she had them all well tucked in and prayers had been silently said, she returned to the man still sitting by the fire.

II

The storm out there had not slowed down yet and the old wolf had not reached his destination. A few more rocks to climb and then the last challenge: a five-foot leap to the top of a big, flat, mossy rock that decked the small triangular entrance of a little cave carved into a bank that overlooked a deep canyon... across, as if designed by The Divine: a steep wall, magically terraced with impressive sculptured rocks nesting many lush communities of firs, pines, sassafras, wild cherry, vines, ferns, grasses, and all that could fit in.

The trees were all gently bowing to the southeast where the sun, since ever, had risen within the gap between the canyon walls.

Four, then five steps back, a few fast steps forward to help the jump, a sudden stop, a few steps back, a semi-run, a jump. Now on that familiar deck, that stone platform that balconied the universe, on that spot that meant safety, home, family, he paused for a moment, looked to the right, looked to the left, wiggled his nose to the air, then stepped in; all that he knew, all that he loved, all that he had lived for was in that cave.

Two couples, one with three pups, one other that had just begun their relationship with her being pregnant, a female mature but not old who had stood next to the Alpha since after his first companion had been shot together with her two young pups, and finally a six-month-old male, strong, curious, loyal, already showing true characteristics of a king.

There was a moment of absolute immobility when the old wet, tired last of the Alpha stepped in. Then the grandson broke the silence and stillness of that moment with an impulsive run ending with a leap to the giant neck of the one he adored. The older female got up, approaching the Alpha sideways, head down, sometimes transforming walking steps into a crawl, then back to a walk and a clumsy sideways trot until, reaching to him with head bowed, began to lick the end of his lip. The rest followed her in the same pattern with whining and small growls.

He stood there putting his paw on their backs, their necks between his jaws, growling majestically as if he were giving them his blessings. Then he slowly walked to his sleeping spot, a flat surface carved into the wall of the cave a little above the rest. He lay down with his front legs in front of his head and, as he glanced at the entrance, and his eyes glided over the pack, expelled a deep breath lowering his head over his

4

front paws, his eyes stayed open for a while in deep thought, then his eyelids slowly lowered into a deep sleep.

Out there the furious storm had silenced the menacing sound of its wind, its thunders and the violent landing of its rain; perhaps it too found a place to rest, a den out there deep in the midst of the universe.

It was not long till the first golden ray came into the cave through the entrance to announce a new day. The three pups and the little Alpha were playing outside the den from before daybreak. They played "hunt" and wrestled with one another heartily; they played as if it were not play; to them it was real. They were testing their strength, they were experiencing firsthand fear and courage, they teamed together to catch a mouse. They did not think of anything but the moment. They had not a past and they never thought that there would be a future. A few squirts of their mother's milk for some of them and a regurgitated meal for those who had lost their mothers were all they needed. The sun had now lost the shades of gold. It was blunt and indiscreet, it was doing its job, it was warming and drying the land, it was calling back to the sky the water it had shared with all.

For the adults the new day meant new challenges. They did have and remembered a past, a very recent past, a past that lasted a long time, a past that had given them experiences and wisdom, but a past that unlike any other past could not give a cure or a solution for the maladies of this present.

As far as they remembered there was only one way: They always had an Alpha, they always had to dig or find a den, they always had to mind territory, they had to continuously perfect hunting skills, they had to know how to survive winters, they had to know how to find and keep a mate. They knew how to use strength to protect and raise the next generation.

None of that past, none of those experiences could help to overcome, to bypass this unexpected present, this thief in the calm of night, this change that left them in a chilling perplexity, but still with a spirit that could never ignore the propelling force of that ancient mandate of old still echoing in their hearts: "Go multiply and replenish the earth." They had found themselves running endlessly to exhaustion hoping to hunt, hoping to eat, hoping to run back to their den with a sense of victory and fulfillment.

The irreconcilable sound of shotguns was to them the sound of death. They were starting to parallel that sound with that new strange man. Every time they encountered one of them they heard the loud sound and immediately after, one of the pack was left behind bleeding; not a chance to fight, not a challenge, not an opportunity for the pack to help.

This present reality was unheard of; it defiled the very laws of nature. This new present left them emptied and broken; the way they ran, the way they walked was different; it was as those who had lost confidence. Their strength, their fighting skills, the few laws of nature that they always could count on were now useless, obsolete.

The buffalo had become scarce, the moose more difficult to find, those strange humans had become more numerous. It seemed as if they were commanded by a dark powerful force, a diabolical power that was able to eviscerate man of the very core that makes a human a human: the soul, the mind, as if, once deprived of that, they were filled with a senseless, voracious destructive force that made them unable to stop destroying all that they could: animals, trees and even other humans who till now had been living in harmony, sharing the bounty of the earth equally.

There was a rumor among the living things of the forest, sea fowls and even the trees that dwelled along the coast that they had seen them, had seen this new human arrive in monsters that swept over the water, propelled by huge wings flopping in the wind, a rumor that the buffalo that once ran wild and free were often found lifeless, piled up in hills of carcasses.

Grandpa, the old Alpha, had to think of a way to survive, a way to lead his pack to a safe place, safe from the danger of this destructive force, from this spreading fire, this plague that seemed like the beginning of an apocalypse.

His mind began to transform. It was beginning to experience the metamorphosis of those minds that are moved by life's difficulties and dangerous events. It was the awakening of the inner being that senses life-threatening situations, the instinct of those who survive, the spirit of leaders who commit never to accept defeat. Things had to change, pleasant things had to be sacrificed to avoid the worst, all had to be left behind. His scent, his strength, his instinct was all he had to take himself and the rest out of this affliction. They needed to climb higher on the mountain; winters were going to be harsher, a new territory needed to be claimed.

Things would have been a lot easier if all this had happened at least five years ago. The weight of his age was becoming more and more undeniable to himself and somewhat obvious to the pack. He knew he was running out of strength and sooner or later he would have to deal with the challenge of a stronger younger male. He secretly hoped that the one-year-old grandson, furnished with ancestral royal blood, would be the one to succeed him.

But for now the old Alpha was still strong and respected, so there was not time to waste. They had to leave their territory behind and begin to climb higher on that mountain now. The others had no idea about this decision till the old wolf, with intimidating growls, aggressively in a demonstration of power and strength, began to press his body weight over each one, showing his fangs, holding their heads between his jaws. They all abandoned themselves with gestures of surrender and reverence, except one of the older males, the father of the three six-month old pups who, for an instant, attempted to react. The Alpha's growl prolonged and became louder, the weight of his strong body pressured on him with more intention and determination, his powerful jaws tightened their grip until the young wolf gave a sign of submission. The Alpha let go and began to run uphill. The pack followed, knowing that something serious was happening and there was no room for perplexities. They ran for a while, then their run became a trot, and after a while a walk.

The night had fallen again upon the earth. There was a sense of safety in the dark of the night, they could not be seen as well. It seemed as if the Alpha had picked up a scent. Yes, it was the scent of a moose. They all began to follow that scent; it was the best smell they had smelled for a long time. They knew it was a weak and struggling moose; it was going to be an easy catch. Soberly and cleverly they followed his tracks for a while, then there he was. They did not take long till they had him down.

After the abundant meal they lay around for a while, then after munching on some leftovers began walking uphill again. The Alpha had to find a new place to settle, perhaps a place where the deathly sound of shotguns would not be heard, where water and food would be available. It was at dawn when, as the sun was unblanketing the earth, that the Alpha noticed a hidden entrance into something right behind a rock. He stopped for a moment to sift the scents of the air with his nose, perceiving no danger. Down below the slope an indentation in the ground was holding water.

Everyone was feeling the same; this place seemed tranquil, and so far had no territorial problems. The old wolf approached the new small cave. The entrance could hardly be seen, being almost totally covered with a very thick vine of Japanese bittersweet competing with a wild rose, both exhibiting their invaluable and colorful fruit, a sign that winter was near. The Alpha smelled and looked through the vines; the cave was empty and probably had been empty for a while. His tail waved; the others came closer as they sniffed around cautiously. One by one they all made their way through the vines into the moist dark cave. They all rested for a while, then they became playful till the sun lowered again behind the mountain. Then the males, including Prince, ran off into the wilderness exploring, marking territory and hunting. They did that every night and every night they were able to eat.

III

A few months went by. The universe had been merciful to them. They had been eating sufficiently, they felt free and fulfilled again, but sadly from afar at times you could still hear the echo of that sound that had forced them to leave it all behind ripping through the silence of the mountain: a reminder that persecution was not yet over.

It was an early morning when Grandpa was sitting gloriously at the edge of the cliff on a rock, a spot from which the eye could travel endlessly. He sat there often to think and observe. That morning a chill was softly declaring winter standing at the door.

Prince ran to join him, sat closely next to his idol. They did not look much different in size anymore; they were almost identical except for the angular shape typical of a youngster, a big difference from what seemed only yesterday when the old wolf daily vomited his prey at his tiny muzzle and lay over him in the night to keep him from freezing.

Now, sitting next to him shoulder to shoulder, Prince could feel that familiar lifesaving warmth expelling from his body, accompanied by the sound of a familiar heartbeat: a lullaby that had sung of comfort, courage and hope. They sat next to each other for a while. The Alpha never moved his head. He stared far out into the infinite as the young prince periodically turned slightly to look at him, then straight forward to the horizon. From afar, the pack was watching with curiosity. It seemed as if the old wolf were soberly revealing a secret, perhaps a plan, a strategy.

From far above large flurries began to descend, filling the air. Both remained seated shoulder to shoulder for a time. Then, the young wolf interrupted that moment, strangely circled the Alpha a few times with awkward movement, muzzle bucking him gently a few times, then with a most agile movement he sprang off the rock. The firmament hiding behind an immense gray sky, the large but light snowflakes that with suspicion were invading the air, the stillness of the trees as far as you could see, the perplexed look in the eyes of the pack, the unsettled behavior of the Prince, told the universe that a peculiar, profound, unimaginable plan had been given to the young wolf... What was the secret, what had that old wolf revealed in the stillness of that early morning?

Whatever it was, it was buried in Prince's heart and mind. For now, there was no need to reveal the secret. No one would understand it. Even he himself had a hard time reconciling with it. Luckily such an extreme plan was not needed right now. Winter had advanced and enfolded their lives, making things more difficult. A few times they had to fight a mountain lion over food. Grandpa had been left with some injury out of the struggle, but all that was nothing but regular wolf life until...

One morning the cold winter breeze brought a familiar but unpleasant scent to the door. After the first few curious, questioning and unbelieving sniffs, they all simultaneously and believing stood up with erect ears. Their heads in absolute stillness, only their eyes moved slowly left and right. They tried to hear but they couldn't. The light wind had carried that scent from some distance, but the scent was enough to reveal it was man. They all were sure it was the death-spreading man and they knew he could not be too far. Their hearts failed—would they have to move again? Grandpa, the Prince and the oldest of the males slowly walked outside. They looked, they smelled, and their ears moved in all directions to pick up a sound.

Grandpa walked ahead cautiously. The young wolf seemed anxious; from the cliff of the rock the scent was a lot clearer; they had to follow the scent to find out how far away he was and how many there were of them. All the old wolf wanted to do was assess the problem and then become invisible, stay away from that creature. . .hide.

It was not so for the young wolf. He still resented having been forced to relocate the first time. He had left against his will, from the very beginning he believed that they could overcome man with their strength. Now it was happening again. To him it was only a matter of territory; he was not willing to lose that territory to anyone. Three of then walked together, equal in appearance, being of the same species, but intricately charged and propelled by three different energies, three uniquely different spirits:

The Alpha, with the spirit of one who since a young age, when fire was circulating in his blood and impulse was at its highest level, manufacturing an endless river of competing decisions, was equipped with an innate filter that discerned what to let in and allowed to come to pass only those decisions that originated from the desire to bring forth well-being, decisions that are prolific in the production of a long lasting future, decisions impregnated with the power to deliver a broad future, able to encompass the fulfillment and realization of those with whom we coexist. That filter is the greatest gift of all. It is the gift of wisdom.

The young adult, whose fire running in his veins was the highest authority in decision-making, a fire that originates in the visceral self-trust. It was the spirit of those who, indulging in the bewitching taste of their own present emotion, would acknowledge no one but themselves. He had the spirit of those who are courageous with a diseased courage bringing forth actions that, like uncontrollable brush fire spreads, devastates all, including the one who had started it.

The Prince, with a predestined gift to be a leader, torn between his royal blood and the blood of a youngster that sees no danger running in the same veins. That inner struggle could have resulted in reckless polluted ambition, but he had made the decision to follow and honor the one he trusted. In his instinct he knew that to be a perfect leader one has to first master the art of following.

Now their sense of smell and also their ears were telling them that a dangerous man was very close. It was right there past the small hill in front of them. They climbed up quietly, and lowering their bodies to the ground, they looked behind the hill and there he was!

The Alpha and Prince would have stayed there hiding for a while and then perhaps followed at a distance for a time, but the young adult unexpectedly broke out of their post, running ferociously and mindlessly downhill to attack the man. Touched by that spark of senseless passion and determination, the prince was beginning to run with him, but the Alpha promptly growled him down. At the same time the wolf who had followed his will, halfway to his target became still and bleeding, gasping for his last breath, soon after the loud sound of the familiar deadly shot.

Difficult to say—Is the flavor of that last breath bitter or sweet? Is it a painful goodbye in anguish to life, or is it liberation from the limits and needs of the physical?

Certainly there was no question by observing the old wolf and the young follower running away downhill, carrying on them the unconcealable load of horror, fear and uncertainty that no liberation had occurred yet. Undoubtedly they were tasting the bitter taste of uncontrollable life-crippling events with one and only one sweet, the sweet sentiment made available for the strengthening of the living. . .HOPE.

What was there left to do? Hoping for what? Yes, plenty of things to hope for, but is that the hope that directs your eyes to a chimera? They needed a hope that is steadfast and sure, a hope for a possible way to escape this apocalypse that was dooming them. The trees from south to north, from east to west, in trembling and fear were expelling a lament. The birds who migrate spread the news abroad, the massacre was not only for Grandpa's pack—it was for every existing wolf.

The trees had been spectators of long rows of lifeless wolves hung upside-down everywhere, birds had seen man ripping their skins off their bodies; the sound of proud and frightening laughter was echoing in the wilderness. Man's intent was to bring the wolves into extinction.

Grand and Prince were running toward the den, crossing a small snowy valley. Weakened in the midst of their own tragedy, they could still find strength and some comfort in each other's presence and the sound of each other's breath. They were running across that valley enfolded in a small snow ghost when, like the sound of a whip tearing the silence, a shot was heard ...The old wolf whined and tumbled in the snow a few times, then began to run again. When past the open valley, under the canopy of a thick pine forest, the speed of his run gradually slowed down to a stop. Prince turned around speedily and when near enough, frenetically began to move his front paws over the old wolf's back as if digging. He tried to lift him with his muzzle. In desperation grabbing the fur of his neck, he dragged him for a while, then began anxiously to lick his face, his mouth. Then, depleted, yielded his will to the Higher Power who in His time calls back His own.

Prince sat up straight, lifted his head to the sky, and let out a howl choked with sorrow and anger. The echo of his grief resounded in the firmament, the wind moved a few dark clouds to block the rays of the sun, taking away color from the earth.

Suddenly, almost abruptly, without reluctance Prince turned his back to the calamity before him and began to run faster than before. It seemed as if he had been crowned. He did not take too long to figure it out. He had become the one who had to take care of what was left of the pack.

When he arrived, the pack got up to greet him; they rubbed against each other, licking each other, with ears tucked back and tails down, bewailing their loss. They lay around for days periodically ululating through the day and the night. But even in the deepest grief, the congenital desire for life and victory becomes the predominant emotion, and sooner or later one has no choice but to respond and reach for existence and vitality, the only alternative being to perish in sorrow. It seemed as if everyone in the pack had already accepted Prince as the new leader. So Prince, now King, Alpha Wolf, began to regroup his pack, establishing order and rank. Then those few able to hunt went hunting with him.

To this point Prince had held back most of his gifts. Now he was a continual demonstration of power, perseverance and wisdom.

That day they had an abundant meal and carried some to the pregnant female who soon would deliver. As they were moving away, leaving the carcass behind, Prince noticed a family of coyotes who had not wasted any time helping themselves to some of the leftovers. There were three of them: a male, a female and a daughter, a very young female. He wondered if they were the same coyotes that Grandpa had observed for a while and had often allowed to feast on his leftovers. Had they trailed them uphill from that first territory left behind?

The young Alpha turned to look back a few times; he kept looking at them with curiosity till at the turn of the hill they could not be seen anymore.

The small pack of wolves led by Prince was beginning to heal and rebuild again. The members of the pack felt secure under the new young leader, but Prince was never at rest.

He was smelling the scent of man too often and too close; memory of Grandpa's death next to him was very fresh in his mind and what Grandpa had revealed to him that day sitting beside him on that cliff had never left his mind.

IV

Winter had grown to its fullness, becoming the most dominant force ruling the wilderness. Every living thing had to succumb to it. Its severity kept man away from the mountains and, in spite of the difficulties that came with winter, the pack was able to survive and even prosper. The coyote family kept inviting themselves to leftover dinners and, even though they knew the danger that at any time the wolves could decide to attack, they found a sense of comfort in the fact that for two generations of Alphas they had been allowed.

To the coyote family the wolves' leftovers were a plus and a delicacy, rarely their only means of survival. They were not entirely dependent on that meal but it definitely helped to meet their needs.

Contrary to the wolves who were slowly being exterminated, the coyotes were increasing in number: the more the wolves were exterminated the more the coyotes multiplied. Coyotes were equipped with different skills from wolves. They knew how to become invisible when they had to. They occasionally were killed by bullets or by poisoned meat intended for the wolves, but they were not affected by the diminishing plentitude of larger game, since they could still find nourishment in rodents like mice or moles, also snakes' eggs, small fowl and even insects. Sometimes they would even eat grass, berries and various fruit.

Wolves were much more vulnerable. They were very visible, very blunt, and they mainly relied on the prey that also was being exterminating by men. Because of a lack of proper nutrition and the unceasing persecution, the entire species was being eradicated. It was just a matter of time until all of the race would be annihilated.

Prince and the pack seemed to have received favor and the Grandpa's idea to move to the high country seemed to work, at least for now. But the loss of Grandpa and the impulsive wolf was undeniable evidence that man had arrived and had begun the merciless, mindless slaying, even up there. Winter's strength had slowed down man for just a time, but even winter, as strong and dominant as he was, had to bow to universal laws and slowly retreat. In the air you could already sense the arrival of a new season.

When winter began to take his first steps toward retreat, when the trees, like naked Hercules planted in the Earth, were exhibiting for a while longer their potent trunks and with sinewy but elegant arms were conducting gently the sound of the mysterious wind, when still colors were suppressed, waiting for the moment to explode like a volcano emitting lava dressed as Harlequin, when still at distance winged creatures were beginning their journey to be protagonist and spectators of the grand and magical awakening, at the same time Eros was beginning to roam over the land filling creatures with his spirit to touch their souls and their flesh with passion, with the uncontrollable desire and need to bring new life, new beginnings.

On a late winter day, when the snow slowly began to melt and the snow crust that had made running or even walking difficult was now a soft cushion, Prince began the habit of sitting on that elevation as Grandpa had and a few times, from that observation point, he had noticed the coyote family running across the small valley below. Were they the coyotes that Grandpa had observed when sitting there for those long periods? Was it from that cliff that he formulated that secret plan, that shocking vision for the wolves' future?

As Prince also began to observe them they seemed happy, they seemed secure. One day, as the wolves were consuming their catch the coyote family, with dangerous boldness, approached the carcass a little too soon, not waiting for the pack to move away to a distance, and despite all the generosity that a wolf can have, that behavior could not be permitted. All in one accord began to chase them ferociously. The three coyotes ran for their lives. As Prince was about to catch the young female, unexpectedly she stopped running and began to rub and roll herself on the ground.

The rest of the wolves continued to pursue the two adults while Prince went to attack the small, vulnerable coyote. He pinned her down, belly up, with her whole head in his mouth. He did not squeeze; on the contrary he slowly let go and began to smell her all over, slowly and almost meditatively. She continued rubbing on the ground and whined as she snuck a few licks on his lips. Prince was acting surprised, curious, nearly awkward. In his meditative sniffs he had picked up the scent of a spirit possessed by The Powerful Eros.

The pack was running back. Prince reluctantly and slowly let go of this filled-with-surprises and pleasant prey, then he ran to join the others. The young coy jumped to her feet and trotted to join her parents.

No one was hurt through this experience, but the coyotes had learned a lesson: They could not relax around wolves. Prince and the young coy, perplexed and confused, were beginning to learn a very profound and different lesson: What had been held and believed to be impossible could become possible.

For the next few days Prince was a little restless and kept going back to that high rock, hoping to see her passing by across the valley down below.

The silence of the winter was slowly filling with the harmonious song of birds, the trees impatiently were beginning to show their primal and pale buds. A message of rebirth and vitality was heard and felt everywhere, but in the midst of that burst of life, out of a forest that seemed enchanted with serenity and the magical gift of life, dreadfully, flocks of frightened birds emerged, breaking out from the thick crown of trees, loudly squawking the alarming sound, the crows being the loudest. All the animals of the forest knew not to mistrust the alarming sound of the crow; they were telling the truth: Deadly intruders had infiltrated the forest, polluting the magic of life with the black magic of death.

Numerous men were walking in the same direction, spaced apart in an amphitheatre shape, carrying guns and noise-making instruments: trumpets, tambourines, empty cans filled with pebbles. It was a real expedition to find and kill every wolf left on that mountain. Perhaps the man who killed Grandpa returned to his people telling stories by the fire about wolves that ferociously had attacked him when hiking on that mountain. Was he back with a reinforcement of enthusiasts to eliminate the problem forever, exchanging lucre for life?

Prince and the pack were out hunting, all of them except a litter of three still a little too young to keep up with the rest of the pack, but big enough to be left alone for short periods. The unceasing alarming sound of crows was a trustworthy signal that something very dangerous was approaching. The noise of trumpets and percussion was meant to create panic, to create an environment of havoc and to induce animals to act in confusion to the point where they would run out in the open from their hiding places.

The pack was running together with Prince at the head. The cacophony was achieving its purpose, it was confusing them, making them nervous and terrified.

Then like the sound of a furious storm, a rain of lead poured out on the open valley, wounding and killing whomever it touched. No sound could be heard coming out of the wolves, not one squeak, not a bark, not a whine. You could only see them fall with undignified tumbles; you could see splashes of crimson following them. With total loss of dignity they limped and dragged themselves to their final stop.

Prince's mind was numbed with panic. He kept on running unconsciously in the same direction toward the den, till in a spark of last-minute resolution he changed direction, heading toward a sharp hill covered with big rocks. In there he was less of a target and possibly could get away once behind that sharp pointy hill. One step before the rocky area, the only other wolf left was running with him only a couple of steps behind, and as Prince was making it behind the first rock his only companion became victim of the bullet. After that, as the massive rocks mimicked a scintillating smile under the lead rain, Prince made it to the top.

The loud sound of trumpets, percussion and blasts ceased. Before fleeing downhill and vanishing in the thickets below, the only wolf left, Prince, the Alpha, with dangerous ingenuity, bounced onto the tip of the highest rock to look back for an instant. The sun was shining bright behind him, transforming him into a dark sagoma, a sight that immobilized as if bewitched the small crowd of humans. Their minds were led into more superstitious imaginings, inspiring them to create more mysterious stories. My guess? The title of this last one would be, "The devil in the wolf."

He posed on that rock for a blink of an eye, then vanished in the glare of the sun. When the group of men came back to their normal senses and began to gather their trophies, one of the men, showing a concern mixed with fear and superstition said, "I know what that shadow standing on that rock was; it was the eternal spirit of the wolf who in his time will avenge his own."

A few meditative, consenting, and questioning hums were expelled from a few men standing near enough to hear, then the typical burlesque loud laughter echoed again in the wilderness. The pure white snow was left behind as a mural with abstract images, a message only for those who look closely, only for those who are not afraid to know the truth. As the ball of laughter and the murmur of words without sense, words that smelled of ignorance and greed, rolled down and away from the mountain, silence returned to be slowly filled with the harmonious chirping of birds. Flowering plants continued to press with energy through the lightly frozen earth. The sky remained bright and blue.

There was a refusal to mourn that day. . .perhaps the universe and the creatures therein had decided to rejoice and to lend their attention to that ancient hope, the hope of that day to come, the day when...

"The wolf also shall dwell with the lamb, and the leopard shall lie down with the kid; and the calf and the young lion and the fatling together; and a little child shall lead them. And the cow and the bear shall feed; their young ones shall lie down together and the lion shall eat straw like the ox. And the suckling child shall play on the hole of the asp, and the weaned child shall put his hand on the cockatrice's den. They shall not hurt nor destroy in all My holy mountain . . ."

Down below, behind the rocky hill, Prince stood motionless in a state of shock. Blinded by panic, he had forced himself into a dense, impenetrable thicket of thorny vines. He was standing there emptied, his mouth open, his tongue hanging out dripping with saliva, his eyes without aim floating into emptiness, his chest spastically and frenetically panting to the rhythm of a heart that pumped uncontrollably, not from physical strain, but from the strangling effects of fear.

The sun that framed his silhouette when he posed on that high rock was slowly lowering, nearly touching the horizon, the sky undressed from the limpid bright blue to exhibit the new, elegant, romantic twilight garb. The birds being the main instrument in the sound track of life earnestly played notes of farewell to the light and hail to the night. It seemed as if The Great Scenographer had set the stage, and the Divine Director was guiding Prince to the next scene. So he took the first slow step, untangling himself from strings of vines and thorns, leaving behind traces of fur.

Coywolf

He was held in the stronghold of a past that stubbornly refused to move out of the present, of a hollow abyss left from his loss of now irreplaceable kin and the newly engendered emotion of dejection through the bitter taste of loneliness. He began to walk, breaking the heavy chains of sorrow. Ahead and not too far from him there was his den, and within his den there was his major chain-breaking power: three orphans who had waited all day for the mother to come back with her warmth, with her love, and with food. In the urge to be who he was, in the call to do what had to be done, in loyalty and in the depth of his elemental love resided the antidote to the tyranny of sorrow.

He arrived at the cave and rushed in anxiously, wasting no time to lick them with eagerness. The reunion had nourished and lifted the spirit, but the flesh also needed nourishment. None of them had eaten for many hours. The feeding task, the hunting task, were all up to Prince who, morally and physically depleted, lay down rolled into a ball. The pups did not hesitate to crawl on top of him, next to him and between his hind legs. He slowly stretched a little, making some room. Yes, they were all still hungry, and deep inside they all knew they were lost in a tempestuous ocean of misfortune, but they also felt that in each other's warmth and affection was the island they could rest upon.

V

In the middle of the night, moved by hunger and responsibility, Prince went hunting for the first time alone. He traveled a great distance trailing the scent of a moose, and when it was close enough, began the chase. In vain he tried to pull him down. The moose stopped, kicked him and bucked him away. Prince, aching and humiliated, wisely stopped the confrontation just in time to avoid broken bones. Understanding the limitation of being a solo hunter, he began to look for easier and less dangerous game. Daytime was chasing the night away and he had not been able to find anything to eat, but on the way back to the hungry pups, a miracle: A goose unable to fly was standing near the partially frozen pond just below their cave. No need to say what was for breakfast that morning. For the next few days, luckily but not without struggles and difficulties, Prince had been able sporadically to provide a little here and a little there, enough to silence the demanding voice of hunger, but not nearly enough to provide for their nutritional needs, so every day they were all getting more undernourished and weak.

Nostalgically one day Prince went to sit on the high rock where long ago Grandpa and he had sat, where he had been the recipient of a secret message. That message that then sounded so impossible was now beginning to make better sense and was becoming more appealing. As if to reassure his wondering mind, the coyote family crossed the valley below as usual, happy and well nourished. And even better, the spirit of Eros enfolded the young female coy like an aura.

Every word that the old wolf had said that day was now speedily rewinding in Prince's mind. The old wolf had foreseen this moment and in his wisdom had told Prince to observe the coyotes, how they were able to survive despite every obstacle. He had told him to choose a female coy as a mate to continue the wolf dynasty within the coyotes. If they could unite gifts with them, if they could learn to be invisible, as they were, if they could be able to eat even when man had exterminated all big prey, if the spirit and genes of wolves could be preserved, carried across this muddy flood of persecution and extinction, then maybe one day they could walk into a future of prosperity, victory, and perhaps revenge. That was the secret, that was the plan that had been given to Prince, the plan that now could and had to be carried out to escape extinction.

Prince looked downhill again, his eyes glued on Princess. The possessive, inebriating fragrance that he had inhaled that day when they had come into contact with one another was suddenly and powerfully resurrecting in his nostrils. Like a sailor lured by the song of a mermaid he began to run to the valley. He stopped where the forest met the open field. He stayed there at the edge of the woods pointing at her assiduously, then followed them at a distance. Aware of his presence, the Ma and Pa coyote looked back at him, not understanding his behavior. They were worried and confused. Why would a wolf follow them?

The news of the last wolf massacre was known to all creation, even the rocks who shielded Prince from the bullets. Though they typically are hard of hearing and slow to speak, after absorbing that event, they could not stop emanating the story into the air. They all knew that Prince was a struggling lone wolf.

The young Princess was too young for deep reflection and her body and mind were presently utterly preoccupied in response to her inflamed senses, incessantly demanding quenching. Prince's presence, even at a distance, caused no worries or fear. On the contrary, his presence kindled her desire into a passion that overshadowed any other emotion, blurred the most basic practice of logic.

She was acting strange, she moved spastically, rolling herself on the wet snow, performing sudden springs high into the air. Then she flew over the earth toward Prince to a sudden stop a few yards away, only to return to her parents with shy steps like a child who had been scolded. This dance continued for most of the day. Then Prince disappeared into the forest; the orphaned needed him, they were vulnerable and incapable without him.

It must have been midnight when all the elements of the universe in kindred alliance unified: The night was silver under a majestic full moon, a turquoise cape lowered over the earth, scintillating with light blue sparkles, the forest floor was painted with patches of snow and waving shadows of trees gently rocked by the breeze. All joined in the magnificent symphony of the silence as Prince, traversed by the magic energy of creation, was filled with the passionate determination of lovers that makes them able to walk through fire receiving no harm. He walked a few steps into the open field illuminated by the moon, raised his head to the sky, and howled the notes of want and desire, ululating persistent echoes of his emotions to distant land.

At a distance from across the field one could see a platinum silhouette rapidly approaching. The howl ended; his call had been heard, then with uncontrollable excitement Prince pirouetted around himself frantically before sprinting to encounter her. They met at the center of the valley. Under the heavenly spotlight they engaged in the primal erotic dance, they nipped, they wrestled, they chased one another in circles, then stopped, remaining still for an instant, penetrating one another with their eyes. Then Prince began to run toward the forest. She followed closely, and as the trees clapped hands they vanished in their midst.

Among shadows and splashes of lights in the seclusion of the forest, in a fusion their bodies and souls were melted together. Nullified, they entered a new existence, as if anointed with divine anointment they slid within each other as one, entering a realm of pleasure and love. Exploring each other's bodies, inhaling each other's scent, traversing each other's souls, entwined with intoxicated senses, transported to the most high, in a convulsive tremble they overflowed, becoming to Eros a powerless pleasing offering.

The Prince became King and the Princess Queen, King and Queen of a new race to come, a species germinated in a soil fertile with strife and oppression, a new kind equipped with the power, organizational skill and stamina of a wolf amalgamated with the agility, adaptability, survival, hunting and cunning skills of a coyote.

They stood still for a while. It seemed as if both were in shock, especially King; Queen broke out of her stillness fairly fast and returned to playfulness, but King was only able to take one step or two, as if in ecstasy. A few more steps, a faster few more steps, then slowly as if awakening from a dream, he began to walk, gallop, run! Queen ran along shoulder to shoulder. King had a surprise for his Queen: three hungry pups who would soon be ready to run along in the hunting team.

When at the den it took only a few moments of introduction. Then the motherly instinct and the desperate need to have a mother joined to begin a relationship that was going to last forever. The day after, hunting was the first thing on their minds. It did not take too long for King to realize that Queen was going to be the breadwinner, at least for now.

Along with the addition of Queen to the family came abundant food and nutrition. She knew when and how to catch small game, which was very abundant. She even supplied some eggs when possible. They ate well and with abundance. Malnutrition was a memory of the past, and their present was a prophet telling of a future of prosperity and victory. The three wolf pups grew able to hunt, so now King had some help taking big game, just in time for Queen to begin preparation for the delivery of the first members of the new race.

King and the young wolves were becoming a good hunting team but there were two problems: one, there was not enough large game, and two, they could not repeat history. Becoming a pack of wolves again would only bring back the suffering they had just left behind. They had to learn from the coys, till soon a new generation would arrive ready to carry on the mission long planned and desired by Grandpa.

On a May day came the tender foliage of the trees, the new gentle green of the valley with all the colorful wild flowers, the waters of the ponds now mirrors of the sky, the brook freed from the grip of winter spar-kling over the rocks lifting up a hymn into the air, the birds that had made it through the winter and those that had traveled from the south making music. They all glorified the universe in one accord as the first of a new race was miraculously sliding out of a warm, safe, dark womb into the light. Then one more, and one more came into the light. On that day in the month of May, as the world was going about its usual business, in a secret little cave in the midst of the rebirth of spring, the coywolf was born. Coincidentally they were three girls, a perfect match for the three male pups.

We need to wonder at times if coincidences are co-incidences or if our strong will and desire have the power to make things coincide for the fulfillment of our visions, or if Someone higher is always looking down, micro-orchestrating events according to His will, in His time, and for His good purpose.

It did not take long for the three baby coys to be-come ready to join in matrimony, each with her own young wolf. King and Queen had many more litters.

Man multiplied and continued to multiply and prosper speedily and invasively. Their dwelling places spread everywhere; they could be found in what used to be valleys, along rivers, and on the seacoast every-where. In their blind and voracious hunger for comfort and pleasure they did not consider anything but themselves and what could be of use to them. They advanced, speaking of righteousness and love, and they spoke and thought of a life that would continue in eternity, as they spread death. They claimed to know and to be children of The Creator, as they disregarded all things created.

Among those men there were a few who spoke the language of mercy and compassion, though not fluently. Those few gathered a remnant of the wolf race and in their mercy introduced them to confined areas where they could be controlled and restricted. They put a few remnant buffalo within fences as well, and some of them were raised for meat. Those humans who once had roamed free among the wolves and the buffalo were now also recipients of "mercy," and just before extinction were allowed to live in limited parcels of land as a defeated race.

But those few on the earth who could hear the sound and understand the language of the neutrinos which by the millions were traversing the water, the earth, the sky and everything within, understood the neutrinos' revelation; Man, blinded by pride, was becoming weaker and more dependent. In his senseless, voracious consumption of common resources, in his profound disregard, man made himself vulnerable. He transgressed the universal and fundamental law of harmonious coexistence. In the transgression of that law, the one who coexists with the transgressor is harmed and offended, but in the end, it is the transgressor himself who will perish for the lack of the coexistents he once destroyed.

Now...time swallowed King and Queen and more time came to swallow the three young wolves and their coyote wives. Their descendants became many and flourished, while other species, like the wolf, were reduced to near extinction or kept in captivity. Grandpa's and Prince's offspring, in blood alliance with the coyotes, the new race, the coywolf, remains free and flourishes. The coywolves are of an extraordinary intelligence. They are masters of hunting, they are very secretive, they never congregate in public, and have no fear of man. Mysteriously, they spend a lot of their time near man's dwelling places. They heed and observe man closely, they are learning his schedule and all his ways. Like ghosts they even penetrate into humans' crowded cities, appearing to men like a flash that soon vanishes before their eyes; they are all around man, studying and following him. Man, entirely ignorant of being watched, goes about his daily business.

Mysteriously and cleverly, they never take their eyes off man. Why? Why are they so persistently observing man and learning man's way so accurately? Why did they decide to dwell at the margins of man's society? Was Grandpa's plan a plan of survival or was Grandpa's plan a plan for revenge and victory? Was the spirit of the great Alpha wolf equipping the coywolf with the patience of the ancient hunter spirit who follows weakened prey? Is the coywolf's instinct perceiving in man the scent of a perishing prey? Do the coywolves know that man is at his falling stage? Does humanity know that they soon may be taken by a predator who followed and waited so long?

About the Author

Ever since his childhood in his native Sicily, Antonio (a.k.a. Madly Loved) has led a life filled with contrasts. A boy who appreciated what his city life had to offer, he nevertheless often felt compelled to wander off, alone, to commune with nature. A physical fitness buff who worked out regularly, Antonio was also a musician, playing bass in a band he himself started. An avid reader who might be found reading five books at once, he dreamed of being a farmer.

As he grew, Antonio's interests increased. At one time or another he was a professional boxer, a professional dancer, the founder of a theater group, and, of course, a writer.

Later, a sense of adventure led Antonio away from home and to London, Athens, Beirut, Cairo, Damascus and beyond, where he worked as a dancer, and finally to New York, where he opened two restaurants and later a dance/aerobics studio, simultaneously managing his uncle's pizzeria.

In his early 30's, Antonio married Maryanne. At that same time he was discovering a spiritual component of his life that guided him to work for the next ten years in the streets and ghettos of New York City, feeding the homeless and helping to rehabilitate women who had fallen into prostitution.

Now Antonio is the creator and owner of a purely organic landscaping company, as well as a husband of twenty-eight years and the father of three. At the same time he is a published poet who writes in two languages, and whose writings have been shared through his passionate readings in the New York City area.

Local Gems Poetry Press is a small Long Island based poetry press dedicated to spreading poetry through performance and the written word. Local Gems believes that poetry is the voice of the people, and as the sister organization of the Bards Initiative, believes that poetry can be used to make a difference.

www.localgemspoetrypress.com

Made in the USA
Middletown, DE
01 March 2019